Noodles

Sheep Security Guard

by SHARON S. O'TOOLE
Illustrated by LESLIE MORRILL

SCHOLASTIC INC.
New York Toronto London Auckland Sydney

To my first editor,
my daughter Meghan.

No part of this publication may be reproduced
in whole or in part, or stored in a retrieval system,
or transmitted in any form or by any means,
electronic, mechanical, photocopying, recording, or otherwise,
without written permission of the publisher.
For information regarding permission, write to Scholastic Inc.,
730 Broadway, New York, NY 10003.

ISBN 0-590-41208-6

Copyright © 1988 by Sharon S. O'Toole
Illustrations copyright © 1988 by Scholastic Inc.
All rights reserved. Published by Scholastic Inc.

LUCKY STAR is a registered trademark of Scholastic Inc.

12 11 10 9 8 7 6 5 4 2 3/9

Printed in the U.S.A. 40

Meet Noodles

The fluffy white puppy shook his head and looked around. He had just hopped to the ground from the back of Mr. Terrill's car. He didn't know it yet, but this was home — the Terrills' sheep farm in the state of Wyoming.

Mr. Terrill's children, Clair and Matt, came running out of the house to take a look.

"Why, he's just like a little white bear," exclaimed Clair.

"This is Noodles," Mr. Terrill said. "He is a very special dog, a Hungarian komondor. When he grows up, his job will be to protect our sheep from wild dogs, like coyotes, and dog packs. Of course, he won't be really grown-up until he is about two years old."

Matt stooped down and picked the puppy up in his arms. "Oh, good! Noodles can stay in my room until then."

"I'm sorry, Matt, but we cannot make a pet out of Noodles. He will live with the orphan lambs for now. You may pet him when we feed him, but he must stay with the lambs so he will learn his job." Mr. Terrill gently took Noodles from Matt. "Next year, this puppy will be big enough to stay with the whole flock. We don't want him to think he's supposed to protect our family. The sheep will be his family."

Mr. Terrill carried the puppy over to the lamb pen. Clair opened the gate, and the three orphan lambs came bounding over to her. Clair laughed. "Molly, Jack, and Jake — meet Noodles."

Mr. Terrill set the frightened puppy down in the pen. Clair shooed the lambs back in and closed the gate. The three lambs sniffed at the little puppy curiously. Noodles was two months old. The lambs were a month younger, but the puppy was still a little smaller.

Noodles tried to creep away, but the pesky lambs followed him.

Matt laughed. "It looks like Noodles needs to be protected from the lambs, not the other way around!"

Mr. Terrill looked at the shivering ball of white fluff. "He does look like a polar bear, Matt," he said, " — a little, cold polar bear. But he'll be all right. Noodles comes from a long line of guardian dogs. His grandparents protected sheep from wolves in Hungary. His father works on a goat ranch in Texas and hasn't lost a kid yet."

"But he's such a baby," cried Clair.

"Don't worry," her father told her. "He'll grow up into a big dog in no time. Let's go get some lunch and leave the animals alone to get acquainted."

New Friends

The little lamb called Molly began nibbling on Noodles' ear. Noodles backed up and yipped at her as if to say, "Hey, cut that out! Your teeth are sharp!"

Jack and Jake trotted up to take a closer look at their new friend. They were twin male lambs, or rams. Jack's short curly fleece was snowy white, and Jake's was pure black. Molly, the ewe, or female lamb, was a lovely silver gray.

The sheep on the Terrill farm were a "spinning flock," raised mainly for their wool. Mrs. Terrill liked to make beautiful yarn out of her sheep's wool, to knit it into sweaters and hats and scarves. She knew that some spinners liked to use white fleeces, and then dye the wool a rainbow of colors. But she never dyed her yarn.

She preferred the natural browns, grays, and blacks, so she raised sheep of different colors.

Molly's mother had a fleece that was the same beautiful silvery color as Molly's wool. It was Mrs. Terrill's favorite fleece. Not only was it a lovely shade, but it was long and strong. The wool was easy to spin.

Not every lamb had the same color wool as its mother. Molly's twin sister was a snow-white lamb, like Jack.

Molly, Jack, and Jake were "bum," or orphan, lambs since they didn't have mothers to raise them. The twins' mother had died soon after they were born, and Molly's mother hadn't had enough milk for both of her lambs. The Terrills had decided to take Molly away so she could get enough to eat. Three times a day, Clair and Matt would come to the lamb pen, and feed each of the lambs a bottle of milk.

The three bums had no fear of people or dogs as the other sheep did. They figured Noodles was another lamb, like them — though Molly thought that, for a lamb, Noodles smelled a little funny. He certainly tasted funny! She took another nibble at his ear.

Noodles yipped again and crawled under the wooden feeder the Terrills used to give the lambs their grain. Molly could not reach him there, so now he was safe.

Lessons

It wasn't long before Noodles and the lambs became fast friends. He wanted to play with the children, too. But they only patted him and said, "Good boy!" when they came to give the lambs their bottles.

By this time the lambs had come to think of Matt and Clair as their mothers. One day, soon after Noodles arrived, the pup pushed open the gate of the lamb pen. The lambs spotted Clair and Matt playing on their front porch and ran right up to the house.

"What's this?" cried Mrs. Terrill when she saw the three lambs and the white puppy near the front door. She chased the animals back to the pen. Clair and Matt thought it was very funny to see their mother running after the frisky lambs.

"I ought to put you in there with them," she told her children with a smile. "Next time be sure the gate is really fastened."

The lambs were Noodles' only playmates. He was not allowed to play with the other dog on the Terrills' farm — Snip, the Border collie. The medium-sized black and white dog had sniffed noses once with Noodles through the fence, but the Terrills shooed him away. They didn't want Snip around the puppy or the lambs.

Snip was not a guard dog like Noodles. His job was to round up the sheep from the pasture when it was time to bring the flock into the corral.

Noodles peeked through the wires of the lamb pen and watched Snip at work. First Mr. Terrill called to Snip. Snip raced out in a big circle around the flock.

The ewes, which had been peacefully grazing only moments before, looked sharply

at the fierce little Border collie. "Maaa, maaa," they called their lambs, and soon the whole flock of thirty or so ewes, trailed by jumping and kicking lambs, headed for the corral.

Noodles couldn't understand why the sheep were so quick to obey Snip or why Snip would want the ewes to go ahead of him. Noodles was content to stay around the pen with his new lamb friends. They certainly weren't afraid of *him*.

Almost every day, Mrs. Terrill came to take Noodles for a walk. One morning, after the puppy had already been at the farm for six weeks, Mrs. Terrill patted him and said, "You're growing up, Noodles. Before the summer's over, you'll be as big as I am!" Noodles was already larger than the lambs.

As soon as Mrs. Terrill let Noodles out of the lamb pen, he tore around the barnyard for a few minutes. Mrs. Terrill let him run, then commanded him, "Heel!" Noodles had learned that this meant she wanted him to walk by her side.

Noodles followed along as Mrs. Terrill went about the pasture to check her sheep. As they walked along the fence, the puppy suddenly took off for a run. "No, Noodles! Come back! Heel," Mrs. Terrill called. Noodles was confused. He wanted to check out all the good smells of sheep and other animals in the pasture. He wanted to explore! But he obeyed Mrs. Terrill. Soon they returned to the pen. "Good boy," Mrs. Terrill said. "Stay." She closed the gate and left.

Molly and the twins ran up to greet him. Noodles licked the lambs all over their woolly faces, and then they all settled down for a nap. As usual, Molly slept right next to Noodles.

A Mystery Solved

After his walks with Mrs. Terrill, Noodles was hungry. Even though Clair and Matt thought the pup looked almost like a lamb, they knew he needed different food. The lambs eagerly drank their bottles of milk. As they grew, they nibbled more and more on the grain in their feeder and on the fresh green grass that grew all around.

Noodles sniffed at the grain sometimes and even nipped at the grass. It was clear he didn't find it tasty. He shook his head as if to say, "How can those crazy lambs eat this stuff?" But like the lambs, he was a growing baby and loved milk. When Clair and Matt brought bottles of milk to the lambs, they gave Noodles dry dog food with milk on it. He loved this meal.

Noodles was fed in a special corner of the pen. Mr. Terrill had put a wooden panel across the corner. Clair and Matt were supposed to put Noodles' milk and dog food behind the panel, out of the lambs' reach.

One day Matt had set the pan near the edge of the panel. A few minutes later, Clair looked down and noticed that the pup's dish was empty. "Hey, I thought you fed Noodles. He doesn't have any food!" she called to her brother. Matt looked puzzled.

"I did feed him. He must have eaten it all," he told Clair.

"But we just gave the lambs their bottles. How could Noodles have eaten all his food so quickly?" she asked.

Noodles was staring sadly at his dish. Then Molly walked up and pushed him aside to lick the last drops of milk from the bottom.

Clair and Matt laughed. The mystery was solved! Matt had set the dog food pan too near the edge of the panel. One of the lambs must have stuck its nose under the narrow space at the bottom of the panel and pushed the pan out far enough to eat from it. The lambs gobbled all the pup's food before anyone knew what was happening! Even though Noodles didn't like what the lambs ate, it was obvious that they loved his food.

Clair and Matt didn't tell their mom and dad. They got Noodles an extra big helping of puppy food and poured lots of milk on it.

When they put the pup's dish back in the pen, they made sure to set it way back in the corner. Noodles scrambled over the panel, relieved that he wouldn't starve before supper. Molly, Jack, and Jake poked around the edges of the panel, but Clair and Matt knew that the lambs, with their slick hooves, couldn't reach the dish or climb the panel.

A Sad Day

The summer days passed, and soon the trees on the Terrill farm glowed with autumn colors. One fine fall day when Clair and Matt came to feed the lambs their bottles of milk, Noodles could sense that something was wrong. The children's eyes were red from crying. Noodles wanted to make them feel better. He jumped up, put his forepaws on Matt's shoulders, and began to lick his face. Noodles was six months old and didn't know how big he had gotten. He was so heavy he knocked Matt to the ground. Matt howled.

Clair dropped the milk bottles and rushed to help her brother. She grabbed Noodles' collar, but she did not need to pull him away. Noodles felt very bad for knocking down Matt and stood quietly with his head down.

"Clair," cried Matt, "the milk!" Molly, Jack, and Jake didn't understand that everyone was feeling sad. They only knew that the black rubber nipples had come off the bottles, and their milk was running onto the ground. They were pushing each other and trying to slurp up the milk as it bubbled out of the bottles. Jake didn't see Matt and he stepped right on him. Matt wailed even louder.

Mrs. Terrill came rushing into the lamb pen. She saw her children's sad faces and the spilled milk, but she knew they were not crying over the accident. She picked Matt up and put her arms around him. Clair came over for a hug, too. "Clair, Matt," she told them, "now you can see why we got Noodles, and why his training is so important."

"But why did the coyotes have to kill Molly's sister?" asked Clair. "And the gray twins —

the coyotes weren't even hungry. They just left them there!"

"A mother coyote was probably teaching her pups how to hunt," Mrs. Terrill explained. "Now it is more important than ever that Noodles learn to guard the sheep. When he is big enough, the coyotes will be afraid to come here."

Noodles, lying among the bum lambs, did not seem very fierce. He looked through the wires toward the sheep pasture. He could see Molly's mother, with the beautiful silver fleece, nosing the still form of her lamb. She was bleating softly. Farther away, he saw the gray lambs. Often he had watched these lambs bouncing and playing. Now they were lifeless as well.

Noodles felt his instincts stir. When he grew to be a big dog, he would be able to keep the coyotes from chasing and killing the defenseless sheep. They could grow wool and raise lambs but could not run fast and bite as he could.

Penned Up

The coyote attack changed the routine on the farm. Now the Terrills brought the sheep into the corral at night. Noodles could hear the ewes bleating unhappily. They did not like being penned up, for they could not spend as much time grazing.

The days were getting shorter, though. The ewes were nervous about the coyotes, which they could hear howling at night. The sheep soon accepted the change and started heading to the barn on their own each evening. If a stubborn ewe and her adventurous lamb did not wish to come to the barn, Mr. Terrill would send Snip, the Border collie, to bring them in. The sharp stare of the black and white dog soon changed their minds! They ran to join the rest of the flock and Noodles.

Noodles and the bum lambs were now with the rest of the flock. The lambs no longer got bottles of milk, but ate hay and grain with the other sheep.

Many of the mother ewes did not like having Noodles penned among them. They stomped their front feet at the white dog, warning him to stay well away from their lambs. The wise old ewes had had many experiences with dogs and coyotes, and their instincts warned them that they should keep away. "A dog is a dog," they seemed to tell each other, "no matter how much he may look like a sheep."

The ewes stared curiously at Molly when she and the orphaned brothers snuggled up to Noodles in the barn at night. Now he was larger than the lambs and they liked the warmth of his fluffy body. Sometimes Noodles tried to make friends with the other lambs, too. He sniffed their noses and licked their faces, until an alarmed mother rushed over to stomp her feet at him.

But as the nights grew colder, more and more lambs came to join the bums as they cuddled up to the big pup. After a while the ewes could sense that Noodles would not harm the lambs. They started to put up with him and from then on hardly thought of him as a dog at all.

Sometimes Clair or Matt came out to the barn with their father when he checked on the sheep before bedtime. "It's hard to tell which is Noodles," Clair said one night. At the sound of his name, Noodles' head rose up from the tangled pile of wool and fur. The Terrills laughed.

When Noodles saw that all was well, he put his head down and went back to sleep.

More Lessons

Winter came.

Mrs. Terrill sold the lambs she didn't want to keep. The mother ewes and remaining lambs, who were now nearly as big as their mothers, spent their days around the corral. They could not go out in the pasture now because of the deep snow. The coyotes still came around, though. At night Noodles could hear them howling their long, lonely "Oooooo." Each day, the Terrills came to put alfalfa and corn pellets into a special feeder for the sheep to eat.

"Mom says she doesn't want any of this feed to fall into the fleeces," Clair told Matt. "She says it makes the wool harder to clean and spin."

Matt looked at Noodles, who was now nearly as big as the smaller ewes. "It's a good thing we don't have to clean *his* fur," he told his sister. Noodles' once-fuzzy coat was starting to look like short strings. "He looks like Mom's rag mop, with straw in it."

"Dad says his coat will form into cords, which look like skinny ropes. He says Noodles will still have soft fur underneath, to keep him from getting cold," Clair said.

"Yeah, and to keep the coyotes from biting him." Matt bared his teeth and growled at Noodles, like a fierce coyote or wolf. Noodles just walked over to Matt and licked his hands. Matt and Clair laughed.

"Some guard dog you are," Clair told Noodles.

Noodles could act fierce, though. Every time a stranger came to the farm, Noodles barked loudly. When the Terrills told him, "It's okay, Noodles," he would settle down.

Even though Noodles sometimes acted like a big guard dog, he still liked to run and play. Once he tried to wrestle with Molly, as he had with his brothers and sisters long ago. Noodles was ashamed to see that he had made Molly's ears bleed with his sharp teeth. He remembered how she had nibbled on his ear on his first day at the Terrill farm.

Mrs. Terrill was upset when she saw Molly's ears. "Noodles is a puppy," she told Clair and Matt. "He wants to play, but he must not be allowed to play with the lambs anymore."

Once again, she took him out to the barnyard for a romp. She practiced commands, such as "Come" and "Stay" with Noodles. When the play and training session ended, they went back to the corral.

Mr. Terrill gave Noodles an old boot to chew on. "Here, Noodles," he told him. "Chew on this instead of your friend Molly."

Changes

Finally the days began to grow longer, and the snowdrifts were melting. Molly and the other Terrill sheep were eager to be turned out into the pasture again to taste green grass. They enjoyed the sunshine, but it was not yet time to go to the meadow.

One sunny day, Mrs. Coats, a neighboring farmer, came to the Terrill farm in a pickup truck.

"I need two rams for my flock," she told the Terrills. "I hope to get some nice lambs for my children's 4-H project." Soon Jack and Jake, who were now nearly grown, had been loaded in Mrs. Coats' pickup. Noodles and Molly watched through the fence and wondered where their friends were going.

In a few days another pickup pulled into the barnyard. "What could *this* be?" Noodles wondered.

Noodles was tied up, and the sheep were moved to another pen. He barked loudly to let everyone know he was worried. He heard a loud clattering noise. He could see Clair and Matt going in and out of the sheep's pen. What could be happening? Where was Molly?

The noise seemed to go on and on. Finally Noodles laid down and put his head on his front legs. When Mrs. Terrill came, he leaped to his feet. She untied Noodles and petted him. "Perhaps we should shear you, too," she laughed.

Noodles looked surprised when he saw Molly and the other ewes. Their fleeces had been cut off! Molly's beautiful silver coat was gone, and her skin was almost bare.

"Don't worry, Noodles. Molly won't get cold," Clair said with a laugh. "She will grow another

fleece. Mom has the sheep sheared every spring. They won't look so bald in a couple of weeks."

When the shearer left, Matt and Clair helped their mother clean the straw and dirt from the raw wool. The cleaning, or "skirting," reminded Matt of when his father would shake the dirt and grass off Matt's clothes before he let him into the house.

Next Mrs. Terrill combed the wool with a special tool that had hundreds of tiny, sharp teeth. The combing, or "carding," pulled the fibers into straight lines. Carding reminded Clair of the mornings when her mother would brush her hair until all the tangles were gone.

All the wool had to be skirted and carded before Mrs. Terrill could spin it into yarn.

New Lambs

Clair noticed that Molly's mother and the other ewes were growing fatter as the days grew longer and warmer.

"I think we'd better get the pens ready for lambing," Mr. Terrill told his daughter. "It won't be long now."

Mr. and Mrs. Terrill spent a busy day setting up wooden panels. Soon the barn was filled with a number of small wooden pens, called "lambing jugs." The Terrills stocked the shelves with lots of things that Noodles hadn't seen before. There was iodine, for cleaning the navels of the new lambs, and syringes and medicine, to give the lambs shots so they wouldn't get sick. Noodles also spotted something familiar — a clean bottle and lamb nipple for lambs who needed extra milk.

Sure enough, Noodles soon heard a small bleating sound in the corner of the corral. He went to check and found a ewe called Old Brownie licking and calling to two wet lambs. One was already trying to stand. Noodles went over to sniff the lambs, but Old Brownie stomped her front feet at him. She made it clear that Noodles was not welcome anywhere near her new lambs!

Noodles sat down and cocked his head. He only wanted to help! He jumped to his feet when he heard a voice.

"Well, what have we got here?" asked Mr. Terrill. "Clair, put some fresh straw in that pen over there. Matt, run to the house and get your mother."

Mr. Terrill gently picked up the newborn lambs, and carried them to the fresh straw bed that Clair had made. He laid the newborns

down. Old Brownie followed them right into the small pen. Mr. Terrill closed the gate.

The Terrills planned to leave the new family in the jug for a few days. When the lambs were strong and knew their mother, they would be put into a larger pen with other new lambs and their mothers.

Noodles saw Mrs. Terrill follow an excited Matt into the barn. She was carrying a bucket of fresh warm water. "Drink this, Old Brownie," she told the ewe. "It has molasses in it to give you energy." She helped the lambs nurse so they would grow up big and strong.

Spring Again

Soon the jugs were full of new lambs. Better yet, the days were warm, and the pasture was turning green.

"When the lambs are a little bigger, we can turn the sheep out into the meadow again," Mrs. Terrill told Clair and Matt.

Before long, lots of lambs were bucking and playing around the corral. One of them, a frisky white lamb, belonged to Molly's mother.

"I was hoping for another silver fleece, like Molly's," Mrs. Terrill said, "but I'm glad she is a strong, healthy lamb."

Matt and Clair were busy again with two new orphan lambs. The lambs' mother had triplets, but she was an old ewe, and had only enough milk to raise one lamb.

Mrs. Terrill made sure the two bums had received "colostrum," the creamy milk that first appears after a ewe has a lamb. Colostrum protects lambs against many germs and diseases, and a lamb that drinks this rich milk is healthier. Mrs. Terrill had milked some colostrum from a ewe that had lots of milk and only one lamb. She saved it in the freezer until it was needed by the new orphans.

Noodles usually stayed with the flock, although now that he was a year old and as big as the ewes, he could easily jump into the bum lambs' pen to check on them and lick their faces. At night he always slept curled up next to Molly.

It was a lovely day in late spring when Mrs. Terrill came with Snip and herded all the ewes with older lambs out to the pasture. Noodles and Molly went with them. Noodles remembered all the boundaries of the pasture from his walks with Mrs. Terrill. He ran to each corner of the meadow and sniffed. Everywhere he could smell signs of the coyotes they had heard howling on the long winter nights.

That evening, the Terrills gathered the flock and put them into the corral for the night. Mrs. Terrill told her family, "Tomorrow morning, we will put bells on the sheep and turn them out into the pasture with Noodles. The sheep will do so much better if they are not in the corral at night, and I believe Noodles is ready to protect them."

The bells were protection, too. If something bothered the ewes during the night, they would move around and set the bells ringing. The Terrills would hear and come to help.

A Test

The following evening out in the pasture, Noodles heard someone coming. He barked. Then he saw it was only Mrs. Terrill and Clair, bringing Snip out to bed the sheep. They gathered the flock and headed toward a small hill in the middle of the pasture. The ewes preferred to sleep on a hill so they could be aware of any danger around them.

Just as they neared the bedground, a group of lambs broke away. They formed a line and began tearing up and down the ditch bank. Noodles was so surprised that he sat down and looked at Mrs. Terrill. "It's okay, Noodles," she told him as she patted the top of his head. "They just want to play."

After a few minutes, the worried mothers called to their lambs. They sounded just like they were scolding their children. "Come over here!" "It's too late to play." "It's time to go to bed!"

Soon the lambs joined their mothers and they settled down for the night. Mrs. Terrill and Clair said good-night to Noodles and went back to the house, taking Snip with them. Noodles lay down in his usual spot near Molly. He was proud to be given the important job of protecting the sheep.

Noodles did not put his head down and go to sleep. He looked and listened carefully. Before long he heard a strange sound at the edge of the pasture next to the woods. He jumped to his feet and barked fiercely.

"I am a big dog," he seemed to be saying. "Stay away." The noises faded, but still Noodles could not sleep. He paced around all night, making sure the sheep were safe.

Early the next morning, Mr. Terrill walked around the pasture. He was relieved to see that all the sheep were there. The ewes were just getting up. Many of the lambs were nursing. Since Molly didn't have a lamb to worry about, she went off to look for morsels of tender green grass.

In a shady spot, Mr. Terrill set up four wooden panels to make a square pen. He set the big dog's food and water in the middle of the square. "Now you won't have to guard your food from these old girls," he told Noodles. The white dog could easily jump over the panels, but the sheep could not get near his food.

Soon Noodles could see the Terrills out and about, busy on the farm. He was sure the sheep would be safe if he took a nap. He stretched out in the shade under a tree and fell sound asleep.

"Look at your guardian dog now!" Mr. Terrill laughed.

"We didn't hear any coyotes last night," Mrs. Terrill reminded her husband.

Clair and Matt came over to pat Noodles. "You sure are a good dog," Matt told him. Noodles laid his head down for another nap. He knew that tonight he would need to be alert.

Noodles to the Rescue

That evening, Mrs. Terrill, Clair, Matt, and Snip came out to the pasture to gather the sheep. They wanted to be sure that the sheep were together for the night and that no curious lambs were off exploring. Noodles watched closely to see that Snip didn't scare the sheep too much. Soon the sheep were bedded on their hill, and Noodles settled down nearby. Once again they were alone for the night.

A full moon rose, shining on the meadow, the sheep, and the big dog. Noodles heard noises over by the woods. He jumped to his feet and barked fiercely. The noises got louder, and soon, in the moonlight, he could see something moving — a coyote!

Noodles was surprised. *This* was a coyote? Why, she was hardly bigger than Snip. He was expecting something the size of a bear, at least! He growled and ran after her. He was glad to have the chance finally to show that he was tough.

He expected the gray coyote to try to sneak past him, but she turned and ran from the much larger dog. He chased her to the edge of the fence. He was about to follow her through a hole under the fence when he heard more noises behind him. Bells! The sheep! Molly!

Noodles realized that the gray coyote had been trying to fool him and lead him away from the flock. The wily coyote knew that with Noodles gone, the other coyotes in her pack could come in and attack the sheep. Noodles raced back to the flock as fast as he could go. A larger brown coyote had driven one of Old Brownie's lambs away from the others and was preparing to pounce. Could Noodles get there in time?

Old Brownie was stomping her feet at the coyote, but the coyote knew that the ewe couldn't hurt him. He ignored her.

Suddenly the brown coyote heard barking and looked up to see Noodles running toward him in the moonlight. The coyote knew that he was no match for a big dog like Noodles. Like shadows, the coyotes were gone.

All the noise had awakened the Terrills. Mr. and Mrs. Terrill came running. "What happened?" called Mr. Terrill.

The frightened sheep were scattered everywhere, and Noodles was barking angrily into the darkness.

"Oh, no!" exclaimed Mrs. Terrill when she found Old Brownie's lamb huddled alone. "I think she's been bitten!"

Old Brownie went to her lamb and began sniffing her all over. Mr. Terrill picked up the lamb and examined her in the beam of his flashlight. "She isn't injured," he said, "just scared."

"I do believe that Noodles ran the coyotes off," Mr. Terrill added.

"Should we put the sheep in for the night?" asked Mrs. Terrill.

"No, let's give Noodles a chance to do his job," her husband replied.

The Terrills gathered the scattered sheep and stayed with them until they had settled down. Noodles stood nearby. He knew he had a lot to learn about being a guardian dog, but he had passed the first test.